THE WOMAN WHO TURNED CHILDREN INTO BIRDS

THE WOMAN WHO TURNED

DAVID ALMOND

WALKER ❚ STUDIO

AN IMPRINT OF WALKER BOOKS

First published 2022 by Walker Books Ltd,
87 Vauxhall Walk, London SE11 5HJ

• •

Text © 2022 David Almond

• •

Illustrations © 2022 Laura Carlin

• •

The right of David Almond and Laura Carlin
to be identified as author and illustrator
respectively of this work has been
asserted in accordance with the
Copyright, Designs and Patents Act 1988 •
This book has been typeset in Adobe Jensen Pro

• •

Printed in China

• •

• •

British Library Cataloguing in Publication
Data: a catalogue record for this book
is available from the British Library

• •

ISBN: 978-1-4063-0711-5

• •

www.walker.co.uk

• •

10 9 8 7 6 5 4 3 2 1

CHILDREN INTO BIRDS

Illustrated by LAURA CARLIN

A woman came to town.
Her name was Nanty Solo.
She said she could turn
children into birds.

◆

"What rubbish!" said the teachers.
"There's laws against it!" said the police.
"It's just plain daft. It's total trash.
It's piffle, twaddle, balderdash."

◆

"You don't want that to happen,
do you, children?
So stay away!"

But of course there was one little girl.
Her name was Dorothy Carr.
She pretended to be just wandering
and thinking of nothing at all.
Nanty Solo called to her.
"Would you like to sit with me?"
Dorothy knew that maybe she shouldn't.
But oh, she did.

Nanty made marks upon the earth.

She whispered words into Dorothy's ear.

And then she said,

"Go on. Be happy. Off you fly!"

And where there'd once been a Dorothy Carr,

there was now a swallow,

swooping up into the blue.

It didn't last for ever.
Just a few short, soaring minutes.

Soon, Dorothy was a Dorothy again,
heading home again.

"Did you go far, love?"

"Oh no, Dad. Not too far at all."

But she whispered
to the other children,
"It's true! It's true!"

◆

Colin Fox was next to go.
He walked straight up to Nanty Solo.
"Nanty Solo, I wish to be an eagle."
Nanty laughed.
"You'll never be an eagle.
You shall be a sparrow."
She made her marks.
She whispered her words.
Then she said,
"Go on. Be happy. Up you go."
In an instant, Colin was changed,
and off he flew.

Now lots of children wanted a turn.

Even Susan M'Beppe, just four years old.

She became a goldfinch.

Massive, muscly
Walter Pope
turned into
a rook.

Quiet Wolfgang Hurst
was transformed
into a parakeet.

Until one afternoon

the sky above the town

was filled with children who had turned into birds.

"No, no, no, no!"

"Get out of that sky this very minute!"

"Get back down here at once!"

"But what on earth are you frightened of?"

"Time to get rid of that Nanty Solo!"

"She's mad, she's bad, she's totally scary!"

"Bad Nanty Solo! Leave us alone!"

"Vamoose, skedaddle, scarper, scram."

◆

"OK, my dears. I'll be off.

I'm always on the move.

But perhaps you'd like, before I leave,

to have wings to fly

and a beak to sing."

◆

"What a silly crackpot notion!"

"Claptrap, tommyrot, piffle, bunkum!"

◆

"But what on earth are you frightened of?"

Oh look, it's the big feller,

Oswald Malone!

She's whispering her words

and making her marks.

And, golly gumdrops, up he goes!

✦

"Gadzooks, what joy!

Hurrah, what fun!

Come on up! The sky's just grand!"

"Come on, Daddy! Come on, Miss!
Come on, PC Blenkinsop!"
Oh, just look and oh, just look.
Up they go and up they go.

Oh yes it's wild! It's just plain daft!
It's far out, cranky, dippy, dotty.
Nutty, freaky, batty, potty.
"It's glorious! It's just the best!"

Now the sky is filled with joy.

The air is filled with such sweet song.

Up they go and up they go.

Up they go and up they go!

Nobody knows how Nanty did it.

Maybe she didn't know herself.

Soon enough she went away.

She goes to lots of towns they say.

And so that's that.

The story's done.

Go on. Be happy.

Off you fly.